ISBN 13: 978-1-942500-40-7
ISBN 10: 1-942500-40-7

*Dearest Brilliant Brian. -
Grateful me for your book.
I will be forever
& ever grateful
Love & bless you,
Candice Azzara*

God, Please Give Me Patience...and Hurry!

by Candice Azzara & Michael Conley

DEDICATION

We dedicate our "Letters to God"
in this book to the two women
who nurtured us, helped us, and
encouraged us:

Jospehine Bravo Azzara
And
Vivian Mary Conley

Candice Azzara BIO

Broadway actress and comedienne, Candice "Candy" Azzara was born and raised in Brooklyn, New York. She studied acting with Lee Strasberg and Gene Frankel. She made her Broadway debut in "Lovers and Other Strangers" written by Renée Taylor and Joseph Bologna. While starring in the pre-Broadway play, "Why I Went Crazy," she was discovered by agent Audrey Wood (Tennessee Williams' agent) and agent William Liebling (Marlon Brando's agent). Some of her other stage credits include: "Detective Story" starring opposite Charlton Heston at the Ahmanson Theater in Los Angeles and a pre-Broadway play, "Jakes Women" written by Neil Simon at the Old Globe Theater in San Diego, CA, where she starred with Stockard Channing, Felicity Huffman, Peter Coyote, Joyce Van Patten, Talia Balsam, and Sarah Michelle Gellar. Norman Lear saw Candy in a Broadway play and had her flown from New York to Los Angeles to audition for a TV Pilot for ABC called *Those Were the Days*. She got the part. Upon her return to New York, she was cast as a series regular in the CBS sitcom, *Calucci's Department* opposite James Coco. Her agent at William Morris, Marty Litke, said "Now it's time to go to Hollywood." Her many TV recurring roles were in sitcoms: *Rhoda* (Valerie Harper), *Soap* (Ted Wass), *Barney Miller* (Hal Linden), *Who's the Boss* (Tony Danza), and *Caroline in the City* (Lea Thompson). Some of her starring roles in movies-made-for-TV are: *Divorce Wars* (Tom Selleck), *The Christmas Pageant* (Melissa Gilbert), *Final Approach* (Dean Cain) directed by Armand Mastroianni, and *Flight Before Christmas* (Mayim Bialik). Director Howard Zieff hired Azzara for her roles in the feature films "Hearts of the West" starring (Jeff Bridges) and in "House Calls" (Walter Matthau, Glenda Jackson, Art Carney and Richard Benjamin). Some of Azzara's other feature film credits include: "The World's Greatest Lover" (Gene Wilder), "Fatso" (Anne Bancroft and Dom DeLuise) produced by Mel Brooks, "Easy Money" (Rodney Dangerfield, Jose Pesci), "Doin' Time on Planet Earth" (Adam West) directed by Charles Matthau and written by Darren Starr, "Unstrung Heroes" (John Turturro) directed by Diane Keaton, "Catch Me If You Can" (Leonardo DiCaprio) directed by Steven Spielberg, "Ocean's Twelve" (Carl Reiner), "In Her Shoes" (Cameron Diaz, Shirley MacLaine) directed by Curtis Hanson, and "In Vino" (Ed Asner) which was written and directed by Leonardo Foti.

Michael Conley BIO

Michael Conley began his writing career with the distinction of being one of the youngest writers for Bob Hope, penning his TV sketch comedy when he was just 22 years-old (in 1982). Currently, he serves as a Judge for the annual Writers Guild of America (WGA) Awards. As a tenured member of the Writers Guild of America West (WGAW) Publicity & Marketing Committee, Conley enjoys his work to promote the Guild and its members, too. Among the high-profile special projects, he has worked on are: "101 Funniest Screenplays" and "101 Best Written TV Series." A film aficionado, Conley also served as the head writer for the *Hollywood International Spotlight Award Shows* called "A Tribute to the MGM Golden Years" and "A Tribute to the Film Classics." Additionally, he has written numerous gala tribute and variety shows for the American Cancer Society (ACS) to include: "A Tribute to Blake Edwards" with Julie Andrews, Dudley Moore, Rich Little, and the Henry Mancini orchestra, "A Tribute to Arista and Clive Davis" with a Special Musical Tribute by Whitney Houston, and "A Tribute to Motown" with Stevie Wonder and Smokey Robinson. Between his various writing jobs and prior to his work with the ACS, Conley served on the Vatican Press Advance Team as Director of the Press Filing Center for the 1987 Papal Mass of Pope John Paul II at the Los Angeles Coliseum. There, Conley supervised the feature writers, press pools, and journalists from the media networks and international syndicates that came from around the world to cover the historic Papal Mass and visit to Los Angeles. He also received an appointment as a writer in the Medical Media Production Service division of the US Department of Veterans Affairs, where he wrote the training films for new employee orientation and Veteran recruits.

Conley is as avid a reader as he is a writer. As an Account Executive at the public relations firm Pryor & Associates, Conley conceived and executed the LA Public Library Literacy Program with Random House Books and their summer reading programs of the LA Unified School District (LAUSD). For the past 20 years, he has run Conley Communications where he reps numerous A-List actors such as Academy Award nominee Gary Busey (*The Buddy Holly Story)* and TV icon Nichelle Nichols (*Star Trek*) as Lt. Uhura for the 50th Anniversary national tour. He also conceived and executed Nichols' PR campaign for her EMMY Award nominated role on the CBS soap opera, "The Young and the Restless" and its 11,000th episode. One of his special projects is the upcoming 100th Anniversary celebration of the American Legion Hollywood Post 43 to help preserve its Hollywood history. Prior to forming his own company, Conley was Senior Publicist and a spokesperson for the 40th Anniversary of Disneyland. For his entire career, Conley has been blessed to dovetail his scripted writing with his public relations and publicity writing – from freelance writing for NBC and Bob Hope to his regular weekly staff job in the CBS Network Publicity department at TV City. He worked on the PR campaigns for the CBS classic 1980s situation comedies: *Newhart, Alice, The Jeffersons, One Day at a Time, Archie Bunker's Place,* and M*A*S*H. As a journalist, Conley wrote his first cover story for the April 1980 edition of *Photoplay* magazine with a feature story on TV's Newest Heartthrob, Brain Patrick Clarke from ABC's *Eight is Enough.* Prior to writing celebrity interview stories, he had been a California Scholastic Press Association (CSPA) Scholar at Loyola Marymount University in Los Angeles.

INTRODUCTION

Do you hate waiting? I've read so many books on patience. Most of them say, "Be Still...and know." Know what? "Be still." How? "Patience is a virtue." Well, news flash— patience is a virtue that most of us don't have!

We all get impatient waiting at that red light that never turns green... in the endless TSA lines at the airport, the grocery store check out line, waiting at the microwave for popcorn to pop, and the incessant waiting outside the bathroom door while a spouse or sibling is inside doing God knows what! Mama Mia... It's beyond frustrating!

Candy grew up in Brooklyn and I grew up in LA. I'm Irish and Candy is Italian. The journey of our lives also presented us with many comedic moments for both of us along the way.

Candy started her acting career co-starring in the Broadway hit, "Lovers and Other Strangers" which became an Academy Award-nominated motion picture of the same name. Both the Broadway show and movie were written by Renée Taylor and Joseph

Bologna. Candy first starred with Anne Bancroft in the film, "Fatso" with Dom DeLuise and it was produced by Mel Brooks. For decades, Candy also went on to have memorable recurring roles in the hit Network sitcoms, "Soap," "Rhoda," "Who's the Boss" and "Caroline in the City." Candy starred in the CBS sitcom, "Calucci's Department" in New York.

Conversely, I grew up at CBS TV City in Los Angeles where I turned my journalism days at LMU into doing publicity campaigns for the classic CBS sitcoms of the 1980s. I also became one of the youngest writers for comedy legend, Bob Hope, when I was just 22 years-old in 1982, writing sketch comedy.

It's 35 years ago now that I was flying on Bob Hope's private plane to Houston, Texas with John Stamos (when he was Blackie on "General Hospital") and Mindy Cohn ("The Facts of Life") along with a young Jason Bateman ("Silver Spoons") and Justine Bateman ("Family Ties"). We had all been invited to go and be part of a Bob Hope holiday TV special. While they were starring in the show, I was writing sketches for the show. When we got back to

Hollywood, all of our careers took off — the Batemans introduced me to Michael J. Fox and we all became good friends—they grew as actors and I grew as a writer. Michael and his managers had me write black tie variety shows for the American Cancer Society for 5 years. I supported them with my laugh-out-loud sense of humor for 10 years at the tapings of their shows and we became like family!—from Stamos at "Full House" to "Facts of Life" with Mindy, Nancy, Kim and Lisa.

Back at CBS, Phil McKeon and I were at "Alice" tapings where I was his publicist. There were laughs and friendships abounding. They all loved my laugh as much as my writing. Candy and I met in Hollywood through a mutual friend from New York—producer, Paul Scott Adamo. Paul felt strongly that Candy and I would be a great comedy writing team. Who would have thought that her humor and Italian pasta sauce would be the perfect compliment to my humor and Irish potato salad. Uniquely, the comedy we learn in life starts by hearing funny stories at the family dinner table. Food like humor can satisfy even the most hungry of hearts! Our book is full of sharing those magical moments with you!

Candy and I love New York and Los Angeles — from the Brooklyn Dodgers to the LA Dodgers. Whether you have lived in laid back LA or lived in the hustle and bustle of NY, we all have a common connection through our problem with patience!

Life is not always a bed of roses and at times, we all have that human urge to give up and not want to wait for anything. How many times have we all promised God that "if He would only answer this one more prayer, right away, I promise to never do that (thing) again!" Well, instead of being patient, we give God the ultimate ultimatum… and default to the proverbial cliche: "When you're really desperate, go to God."

Most of us expect a quick miracle answer to our prayers because we're taught that God is all knowing; and, of course, we think that we know that He knows just how badly we need that new car or vacation. For most millennials, nowadays, their prayers need to be answered even quicker, too!

They want quick, fast solutions so they don't have to wait too long or wait at all to figure anything out!

Life is not an MGM Musical — it's a rough, tough, enjoyable and sometimes a terrifying journey also. We need to have compassion for each other. One of the greatest gifts in life we have is to share our feelings honestly, so we know that we are not alone and can still find humor in pain and suffering.

We need to express ourselves through our laughter and tears also! Laughing and crying are two of the greatest emotional releases in life. We're all on this journey together. Let us embrace one another and say, "It's Ok, I've been there, too."

From Bob Hope to Anne Bancroft and Mel Brooks, Candy and I were both beyond blessed to have the best of the best in comedy at the crux of our careers on opposite coasts. Candy was born on May 18th which is also the birthday of Pope John Paul II. Ironically, I was selected to be Vatican Press Advance and Director of the Press Filing Center for Pope John Paul II's Papal Mass at the LA Coliseum. While I was preparing to get my Vatican press credentials, Jason was starring in "Valerie" and preparing to become the DGA's youngest ever director when he also directed 3 episodes of "Valerie" at age 18. Jason invited me (and my now famous laugh) to be seated front row center with Justine and his parents in the audience. We both celebrated each other's achievements at early ages in our careers. Now, equally exciting for me is enjoying my many years of being a judge for the annual Writers Guild of America (WGA) Awards. I also received a Senatorial Appointment to the State of California Motion Picture Council and serve on the Publicity and Marketing Committee of the WGAW but nothing compares to making other people laugh.

Still Laughing Out Loud in LA,

Michael Conley

TABLE OF CONTENTS

Letters to God about...

Letter 1

My sufferings as a Mother and Wife

My Sufferings as a Mother and Wife

"God could not be everywhere, so he created mothers."
- Jewish Proverb

You can be a mess and still be a good mom. We are allowed to be both.

Dear God,

This is from a suffering Mother. I've been reading your book. I know you have a son ...but he listened to you. He also said wonderful things about you and knew about respect. He never kept you waiting. In your book it says a lot about children and you give some instructions. Patience with children is much harder than you think. I'm waiting for a phone call from my daughter. She said she would call me at 5:00pm ...it's now 5:30pm. My heart is beating fast, in fact very fast. When she was a baby I nursed her for 9 months ...9 months ...and this is the kind of treatment I get. Like I'm a nobody. Well, I'm a somebody when she needs me to take care of my grandchild. To help her pack and organize her home. I'm a good organizer. She's always on time for friends ...but ...not me. Her own Mother! Mothers are mistreated. Why did she say she'd call at 5:00 or was it 5:30? I'm almost sure it was 5:00. Yes, it is I wrote it on my calendar ...5:00... yep ... here's the proof. It looks like 5 or could it be 6:00? Six doesn't sound or look like 5:00. Anyhow 6:00 would be very

17

late for her to call me. Do you have any idea what I do for her and her lazy husband? This suffering is too much. She married someone just like her Father. All that Therapy and she marries someone just like her lazy fat slob Father. I'm not putting my husband down ...that's the truth. Didn't you or someone say, "The truth shall set you free." I'm sorry but I give up or gave up with him. All these years we've lived in our house and he can't find anything. God forbid if he cooks for us ... he goes on and on as if he slaved for me. His daughter, well our daughter is like that. She's more like her father than she is like me. That's the cross I have to bear on this earth. She said she would phone at 5:00. It's now going on 5:39. This is making my stomach turn. Punctuality! Punctuality is very important. I tried to tell her that and she acts as if I'm torturing her. Why do we have children? Why? For Mothers to suffer? Come to think of it ...your Mother suffered a lot. I love Mother Mary. She's a woman she understands. Now this thing on patience ...Oh, wait I hear the phone ...I'll get back to you.

to be continued....

From a Suffering Mother.

Dear God,

I'm back ...you guessed it ...it was my daughter. She had a lot to do and couldn't find her phone. Her baby was giving her a hard time. He's a stubborn kid ...just like his mother. Well, she did apologize for calling me so late and wants me to baby sit for a week for her. She and her husband need a break and that they have to get away.

She needs a break like a need a hole in the head. This generation is full of lazy kids. I wonder why she didn't ask how I was feeling? It's a me, me and me generation. I said, "I would babysit."

My grandchild is cute, you'd love him ...I love him and he really loves me. He's brilliant ...almost like a Genius. Anyhow, I'll be staying at their apartment. My baby husband will have to fend for himself. I'd rather take care of my grandchild than my husband. Of course I will have to have all the meals made for my baby husband for the entire week. Labels must be put on doors, closets and a guide to what's in the refrigerator on each shelf and the freezer. I'm married 30 years and baby hubby is still helpless. He still doesn't know where the salt is. Then

19

I'll get phone calls from him because he can't find anything. I'm a Mother of two children …My daughter and my husband. Could you give me a break?

Love, A suffering Mother & Wife in Wisconsin

Letter 2

My problems with Mr. Right

My problems with Mr. Right

HELLO
my name is

Mr. Right

Marriage is a relationship
where one is always right and
the other is the husband

Dear God,

First, I want to thank you for my marriage. With a great deal of patience, I waited for Mr. Right...You, kindly, answered my prayers and brought me Mr. Right...we had the right wedding, the right bridal party, the right food, the right flowers, the right romantic setting for our honeymoon. Now, I have a problem...Mr. Right has changed.

I don't recognize Mr. Right. At night he snores ...it's not just a snore ... he sounds like a freight train trying to pull into Grand Central Station. He keeps huffing and puffing and puffing and huffing away...stops for a moment ... then goes on again and again— all night. When I wake up, I look like I never slept. My eyes have bags under them! My nerves are shot and, of course, we want to have children.

Mr. Right now looks very pregnant as if he'll be in labor very soon. He now has a big, and I mean big, beer belly. People are so confused when they see us...they ask. "Aren't you the one whose suppose to have the baby?"

All the years I spent, and all the money on books, and all the lessons on how to have a happy marriage are a load of... you know what!

I'm so confused. Now, with very little patience left inside of me, God, could you tell me what to do?

Love, Mrs. Right in Rhode Island

Letter 3

The Lottery

The Lottery

KEEP CALM AND WIN THE LOTTERY

Might wake up early and go for a run.

Might also win the lottery, the odds are about the same.

Dear God,

Why is it that people who have money...say that money isn't important? But they always want more money, more land, more jewels and more vacations. What do they know? Why are they giving us advice? Who gives them advice?

When my rent is late and my bills are piling up...and my taxes are due...how can money not be important to me?

All these people with all their money tell us to relax and trust. Be patient. It will all work out... Sure they are relaxing on their planes, their different homes...and sailing away into the sunset on their yachts. While they're shining their diamonds and pearls...they say, "Pray, God will provide"...When???

Then I'm told that you shouldn't gamble or play the lottery...but Bingo is OK?!...If I win the

27

lottery, then I won't have to worry about money for the rest of my life.

God, could you help me win the lottery?

Waiting to win the Lottery...
and please make it a big one.

Love,
Anonymou$ in Hot Springs, Arkansas

Letter 4

My problems with cigarettes and smoking

My problems with cigarettes and smoking

Dear God,

Today I made a decision to ask for patience. Patience to wait for my husband to grow up. I had to join a Twelve Step program called Al-Anon to help me to surrender to your plan. Even though my husband doesn't drink I qualify because I have an uncle who is a drunken bum.

Getting back to my husband…he lives in his bathroom and lies like a little kid. I know he still smokes.

He said he quit smoking …that's a lot of bull…His bathroom is filled with smoke and the smoke goes under the crack of the door into every room in our house. The house stinks of his smoke. He insists he quit smoking for his health and the health of our children. What about me???

My patience is killing me. I now leave notes…"Who's Smoking?…I thought someone stopped smoking?" etc.

The Twelve Step program is a spiritual program...and tells me to surrender my will over to a Higher Power...that's you, God. So, I Let Go and Let God.

Now, they tell me I have to work on me. Why??? I didn't know I had to work on me. I mean...doesn't he know that second hand smoke could kill me. He's got the problem. I pretty much got it together.

Love,
Your concerned child of God in Savannah, Georgia

Letter 5

My decision to clean my closets

My decision to clean my closets

Dear God,

Have patience with me…this is my story. I have decided this is it …the end must be now. I cannot go on. Life is much too hard for me. Why are there so many ups and downs…can't it be all happy and sunshine. It's over for me and this world. Why should I go on one more day? Nobody would really miss me. I'm sure there will be people crying for a few days…maybe an hour or two.

But, then they can go on with their lives…and I can finally be rested and at peace. The best way to end it all…I thought … would be to choke myself to death. It was really a dumb choice… it didn't work. It hurt too much. Then I got a knife to stab myself …but I tried it on my hand. The knife was too sharp…that really hurt. Thank God, no blood was coming out of my hand. I wouldn't recommend this kind of killing to anyone.

Then…I thought before I die …I want to choose the dress I will wear when they bury me. My Pink dress will be the best for me…I look pretty in Pink. Now I have to go shopping for shoes to go with my dress. The gold shoes look too cheap. I'll just die if anyone says, "Her shoes don't match."

Now, I have to organize all my drawers and closets. My mother will come in for inspection and go through all my closets. Mom loves to gossip. My closets will be the topic of her conversations. I would be humiliated and not ever able to live with myself if she tells everyone I'm not organized. Please, Dear God, help me to organize my closets. When Mom opens my closets, I want her to be in awe and tell everyone that now she knows that of all the 5 children, I'm really the most organized child in her family.

Now, that I think of it...there's a lot to do before I drop dead. I must be specific about who gets my clowns, lamps, clothes, books, etc. You know my family fights about everything, so everything must be all written down and witnessed because you name it they fight about it.

I never realized how much work I had to do before I die. Let me think about this. Heaven is supposed to be a great place...and if I take my life, I may not get there. I don't want to chance it. God, do you have any suggestions?

What?... Am I hearing you right? You want me to clean out my closets and listen to music...that sounds like good advice. I'll start now.

Love, Your closet-cleaning child in Cleveland

Letter 6

World Leaders

World Leaders

Dear God,

I'm very mad at Adam and Eve. It's such a mess because of them and that silly apple. I like Apples …but to mess up history over an apple is ridiculous…!!!

Since the beginning of time, people in charge continually lose it. They don't make sense. It seems like Everyone who is in charge loses it and messes up their respective industry from entertainment to politics. They all start out saying, "I'm gonna do this and I'm gonna do that… that one said this and this one said that… and life will be easy." Then it goes to their head and many of them become monsters. They want Power and more Power.

Isn't there a saying, "Power corrupts and absolute power corrupts absolutely." Even good people in your book, the Bible, they messed up, too. I really happened to like King David especially with his fight against Goliath, but like all of us, the poor guy, he goofed, too.

The teacher you gave us, the dove, is called the Holy Spirit… right? Coming from Brooklyn, I thought it was a pigeon… I've never seen a Dove in

New York. How do we listen to this teacher? Does it have a voice? How does it sound? Can you have this teacher speak to these leaders?

They sound like leaders who shouldn't be in charge, but yearn for Power. Maybe they'd be better off selling bagels. Can you imagine, Luciano Pavarotti who was born to be a great opera singer and then decided to become a toe dancer with those tights on…jumping and pirouetting all over the stage. The stage would collapse. Well, today's leaders — they seem to be in the wrong business. They're collapsing our country! God, we're in trouble. Big trouble.

Love, an avid apple eater in Austin, Texas

Letter 7

Born in Brooklyn

Born in Brooklyn

Dear God,

My childhood dream was to be part of a family of all nationalities, races and religions. I'm Sicilian, grew up in Bensonhurst— Home of the Jewish and Italian neighborhoods…a real melting pot of families. The waiting and praying was worth it. My entire family looks like the United Nations.

We are different religions and inter-racial and guess what? All we see, feel, and touch is love. Thanks to our beloved Mom and Dad who never judged people by their background or color…You could always hear my parents say, "We're Sicilian." The Italian neighbors would say, "I thought you said, you're Italian!" There is no divide between us.

Sure we disagree on issues …mostly about what we should eat or drink. The Napoli dons say you have to cook your sauce for about 18 hours … My, Dad would say, "They know nothing about sauce— what kinda people have 18 hours to just sit and stir their sauce!" We are a food loving family.

Our love for each other however is so strong you can feel and see it in our dancing eyes, our kisses and hugs as we greet each other, "Hello and goodbye." Once, when I was a kid, I forgot to say goodbye to my Aunt and I never heard the end of it…and I finally had to write an apology letter. What's inside that counts. Our family is driven by this strong energy of love.

There is only one God and you created us all so different so we can learn from one another and have patience learning. So we can look beyond our appearances and see, feel what makes us tick. Listening to the spirit that sweet divine individual spirit within us that teaches us that love …is the meaning for existence.

Thank you so much, now as a really confused adult, somehow, my sweet dream has come true …my family is so different yet so much alike in love. Do you know that I tear up with joy and radiate inside of me when I'm with my family.

Oh, how I wish the whole world was in love with humanity …the precious gift of every human being is a gift to all of us from you. To love and cherish each other …help us to wake up to this powerful emotion of love that truly makes the world

go a round and around. Grateful me for my
international family.

Love, Betty In Brooklyn

Letter 8

My first year of marriage

My first year of marriage

Dear God,

I'm married a little over a year. My wife has become Mrs. Frankenstein… she even hisses like her…but is beginning to look like Mr. Frankenstein. Me, I'm working hard as her slave.

You see I'm part of a band. I play the guitar. When my wife and I disagree, I play my guitar to shut her up. So far, that hasn't worked.

She's from a very large, loud Italian family. I'm a quiet man. You think it was the end of the world because I forgot her birthday…Huh, what…does she expect me to remember everything? I had a gig, I was playing my guitar. If she had any brains, she would know how important that is to me!…And, eventually, "when" I make some decent money, it'll be great for her and she can work less hours at her multiple jobs. I'm not gonna be a waiter my whole life either.

She brings up divorce, every time, I forget to do something. So big deal …I forgot her birthday and our first anniversary. What's the big deal she's not the only one who has a birthday and we're only

49

married a year. I mean who can remember all that stuff. Talk about being sensitive…she cries at the drop of a hat. I'm telling you she's changed a lot…now, she thinks I should be taking out the garbage too!

What does she want from me…? I helped her clean our apartment last month …now she wants me to help her again this month too! She has x-ray vision when it comes to dust. Her life is all about dusting and more dusting. "I don't see any dust," I tell her. She chimes in, "Of course not, I've been slaving all day dusting, Dearie." What's this with the fanatic cleaning??? Why doesn't she just relax …she can't relax…tension is her middle name. All she cares about is how are we going to pay all of our bills! Here I am relaxing watching the game, I quietly say, "Do I look like a Bank?" She chimes in again, and says, "Well, money doesn't grow on trees, you know!" What does she know…I'm right in the middle of a Yankee game…and they're losing…and she cares about all the wrong things. She has no respect for my feelings. I like being with my friends. They're men…Men deal with what's important…things like baseball, football, golf and most important, rehearsal for our band. My wife doesn't like sports. So what does she expect from me? Look I tried …Once I took her to a basketball game and she rooted for the rival team. She goes for the players with the looks, not for the winning team. That was the first and last time I will ever take her to a basketball game.

We did go to a Football game. She enjoyed doing the wave with the rest of the crowd.…but she also asked me so many questions about the players. Who cares if this one is married or single? I couldn't take it anymore. I said, "Watch the game, stop asking so many questions. She said, she heard that one of the Football players was not close to his Mother and that's why they're losing the game. I tried to explain to her, No…he just missed the field goal and that's why they're losing the game.

I now have ear plugs. She doesn't shut up. Maybe we should get a divorce. Feelings…feelings and more feelings…she wants to discuss our feelings. Who knows about feelings? I'm a man. I feel funny discussing my feelings. These women can talk for hours about nothing. That's not for me. My time is used to practice on my guitar. Maybe we should separate…but …I would miss her cooking because she's a great cook. And she does make sure she has my dinner prepared before she starts her job on the grave yard shift. My clothes are always washed and cleaned and of course our apartment is immaculate. Most of all, my Mother loves her and she loves my Mother. In fact, she looks like my Mother. Come to think of it, if she ever really did leave, it would be like losing my Mother. I'd really miss her. We do have a lot of fun together…and make each other laugh.

I should have patience with her. She's kinda cute with beautiful skin. Good skin runs in her family. I can't imagine my life without her. Let me think about this. Being alone is not for me. When we sleep, we cuddle a lot and she is very affectionate. I even like when she snores. Her snores are cute. Patience is the key. I don't want to lose her. Even though she can drive me crazy. I really love her. God, could you give me a clue on how to handle her.

Larry in Los Angeles

Letter 9

Losing Keys

Losing Keys

Prayer is the
key to Heaven, but
Faith
unlocks the door

Dear God,

I lost my keys? I have an appointment with my
dermatologist. Where are they?! I have a pimple on
my nose and I don't want to squeeze it...because it
will leave a mark. I need my keys now!!! Are YOU
listening, GOD? I already prayed the St. Anthony
prayer, "Tony, Tony stick around something's lost
and can't be found." Nothing happened! I still can't
find my keys!

Look, I'm running out of patience and I've had
a lot of patience lately. Ask anyone how sort of calm
and patient I've been (lately). You know in the past
I've not been a good listener and used to cut people
off before they would or could finish their sentence.
Although patience is a virtue, it hasn't been one of
mine. But you should see me now, I've completely
changed. You wouldn't even recognize me. Now,
that I've become more like a Saint, could you
pleeeeeease help me recognize where my keys are?

I promise to keep being a good listener, I
promise I will keep my mouth shut and not gossip, I
promise to be good to all people...forgive me for all

the mistakes I didn't really mean to make (this week). Then, finally I promise not to complain about anything at all ever again…!!!

Let's get back to my problem…about finding my keys. I thought I put them on the table? Well, they're not there. I might've taken them into my bedroom…no…not there. Come on God…where are they? Did I put them on the kitchen counter? There's only the coffee pot on the kitchen counter. My blood feels like it's boiling. Where are they? I couldn't have put them in my purse? Anyhow, I looked there…they're not there! I keep hearing… "Look in your purse again." You know, that little voice that tells me to do things and if I don't listen then I'm in trouble. I'm in trouble all right.

What…Okay, If you insist, I'll dump everything out of my purse. There's one thing I know for sure and my keys are not in my purse.

Oh, My God…well, what'd you know??? The keys are in my purse. I looked before and I'm sure they weren't there. In fact, I'm positive. Is it possible they flew into my purse? How did they get there? Well, thanks again God…and a big thanks to St.

Anthony. I gotta go…remember the pimple on my nose…the dermatologist office closes in 15 minutes…so if I don't make it there in time, could you please make sure YOU get rid of the pimple on my nose? I promise to have patience all the days of my life. Thanks for the keys. Help me to remember you know where everything is. And that's the truth…the whole truth and nothing but the truth.

Love, Key Less in Louisville, KY

Letter 10

Tweeting about Depression

Tweeting about Depression

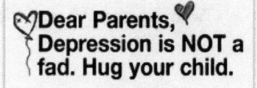

Dear Parents, Depression is NOT a fad. Hug your child.

When you are
down to nothing
God
is up to something

Dear God,

I'm writing to you because I am depressed. I've been depressed for over 30 years…Who in the world created depression?

I'm <u>waiting</u> to get out of my depression and I'm becoming even more depressed waiting to come out of my depression. The problem I have is this…When I'm depressed, I have to create or I'll go out of my mind.

Depression helps me make a good living because I'm an Artist and my different levels of depression help me define and express my innermost feelings; however, happiness makes me too relaxed. I'm not saying, "Happiness is a bad thing. It's good to be happy." When I'm happy all I want to do is go on vacation, hang out with friends, and listen to the birds tweeting.

I'm not talking about "Twitter" when I talk about "Tweeting" although I do like blue birds.

My Doctor said I have a chemical imbalance and that I should take some medication. That means I won't be me anymore. My depression is part of me.

Unbalance is more fun than balance. Opposites attract…so I attract happy people. Short people attract tall people, quiet people attract loud people, unbalanced people attract balanced people. This is my dilemma. I'm still depressed. I'm very creative and productive. I guess I'll have to wait until my depression passes. Change is part of life. This too shall pass.

Love, "Tweeting" from Times Square

Letter **11**

Painting my bathroom

Painting my bathroom

Dear God,

I waited and waited for you to bless me
with a solution to fix my bathroom. Well, I decided to
make it happen on my own, because I couldn't wait
any longer for You. So, off to the paint store I went.
There, I got some plaster. It's called Spackle, but
professionals know the name…it's really easy to use
because it's all mixed and ready to go. Then, I had
the store mix a bright (and I mean) bright yellow
paint…it's so bright, it looks like it can glow in the
dark.

You can tell I'm not a professional painter
and plaster person…because the plaster looks so
lumpy on my walls. How in the world do I get it
smooth? So, I decided to make it look as if it were
part of my design. I thought to myself, I'll create a
lumpy wall effect and that should do the trick. It's an
interesting look— the color yellow that I had them
mix. Between You and me, I think You would really
appreciate my choice. Look at all the colors you
created in the rainbow…some are bright, some not
so bright…well, this is your <u>brightest</u> yellow yet!

Trying to be a pro-painter, I covered some stuff in my bathroom...just in case I would splash some paint. Well, the paint wasn't going on so good especially with the lumpy plaster work, but...it did look different. The color is what got to me...so bright...extremely bright yellow...sunglasses are a must if you go into my bathroom. Well, I was so proud of myself...you see ...I did it all on my time...who needs to wait for God's time, you take forever. Almost part of a wall was painted! Wow! Instead of buying a ladder...why waste time...I've got to get back home and get this done on my schedule. So, I decided to leave the paint shop without buying the ladder.

I figured, why waste money and time when all I had to really do was to stand on the toilet seat to reach the top of the wall...and place the paint can on the seat, too, so I can make it easy to reach. I was almost standing on top of the paint can and it all seemed to be going pretty well, except the paint wasn't going on right. So, I had a great idea...to make the paint go on in circles. There I was twirling around my paint brush painting circles over the lumpy plaster. It was a unique design. I was so impressed with myself that I thought I could start a new creation for all homeowners to use. Now, I became a painter and designer of the "New lumpy bright look."

It was so much fun achieving so much in such a short time. You see, God, I can help You, too. We can all get it done in a shorter time. Well, I didn't realize my toilet seat had a little cushion in it. So, I slipped and kicked the can of paint…there it went flying off the toilet seat…my bathtub was yellow, the toilet seat was yellow…I was yellow…yellow everywhere…except where it was supposed to be. Anyone would think the Sun had landed in my bathroom…Bright…sunshine yellow everywhere.

Thank you, God, that I'm an Adult …because I would've been grounded for at least a year…the mess was…you can just imagine…a bright mess.

Here I am wasting the whole day now <u>cleaning</u> the yellow mess. I've never seen so much yellow...come to think of it, even The Beatles "Yellow Submarine" wasn't as yellow as my yellow!

Forgive me. I should've waited for your time.

Love, Painted Yellow in Yonkers

Letter 12

Getting Sea sick on a romantic cruise

Getting Sea sick on a romantic cruise

Dear God,

I think luxury cruise travel is over rated. Where is "The Love Boat" in real life?

You know, how I prayed for a miracle to go on a cruise for free so I could be really happy. The ocean, fish, my hair blowing in the strong breeze, romance …all on this cruise ship. Thanks to You and Your Mother, my prayers were answered. It all seemed so romantic in the Movies and ads…everyone dancing …hugging, kissing…meeting the one you've waited for your whole life!

This luxury cruise would truly make me happy (I thought) and complete…Like Cinderella or Snow White, I would be happy ever after or something like that. Who knew that I would be sea sick? Too much water all around the ship…up and down, down and up, down and up!

I wish the ship just stayed dry docked. Then, I could enjoy it. Everything and everyone swaying back and forth …back and forth…back and forth. But, the moon was beautiful…there was a moment of elation and ecstasy with me focusing on the moon.

For a split second, I felt romance maybe in the air. Everyone had fun but me. They danced, played lots of ballon games, drank, joked…while I was in the bathroom getting sea sick.

Why do they have so much food on a Cruise? Who can eat when you're sea sick? I wondered where was Mr. Right eating? After all, I took this stupid cruise to meet him! And even worse, where was our romantic rendezvous going to happen? Not in the bathroom…I hope!

Will I ever experience my romantic moment — with my hair waving in the wind and music coming out of nowhere. I believed the stories in the Movies were true. But after being on board, I now know that it isn't true.

All those beautiful ads with the lights on the ships and those cruise magazines…maybe they were just Models made up to look even prettier with the click of the mouse and photoshop.

Why don't they put a warning sign in those magazines too— "Beware you may get sea sick …the ship is not steady…there is a lot of up and down movement…for those with a weak stomach,

71

get advice from your Doctor about coping on the "Romantic Cruise."

When I finally landed near solid ground, I was still weaving back and forth as if I never left the ship. I'm not a fish…fish are used to being in the water …after all, they live there. We, people, are made to be on solid ground…the earth is where we belong. Cement, that's for me… strong solid cement.

Now, I'm finally home from the most **unromantic** trip of my life. In the Movies, yet again, somehow, they all magically unpack their bags and everything is done in a split second just in time for a 7-Course meal. How come they don't get sea sick…or do they? With me, in real life, now comes the unpacking, the washing of everything, trying desperately to get the fishy stinky smell out of my clothes. I am completely exhausted from my sea sick trip.

Thanks for answering my prayers about getting to go on a Romantic Cruise, even though it was a complete disaster. Maybe, next time, You and Your Mother can arrange an Aisle seat in First Class for me on one of those Private Jet services that only the really Rich Celebrities use.

God, while you're at it...Could you make it a trip to Europe...I've never been there. That way, I could walk on solid ground for the whole trip!

Who knows...when I land at the airport, maybe...Mr. Right will be waiting for me and, hopefully, with a bouquet of roses! Yep, Europe will be the perfect destination to bring me all the happiness I am seeking.

So, can you please give me another chance at romance. I read in another travel magazine, Europe is lovely this time of year...and so romantic...with all those different accents and pieces of Art.

Love, Boat-weary in the Bronx

Letter 13

Complaints about the weather

Complaints about the weather

Climate is what
we expect

Weather is what
we get

— Mark Twain

Dear God,

Sometimes, I feel like the weather. Sometimes, I feel like the weatherman— when he reads his weather report wrong, again! The weather is always changing, but I'm stuck in a snowstorm.

Happiness for me is not all the time…it's in moments. Especially when I free my mind of negative thoughts… like "never" — oops, that's even more negative!

So, I took a course on "How to be Happy!" In this course, I paid them and they instructed me to "think happy, wealthy, and successful thoughts and you will become what you think." Well, I was so HAPPY, the Sun even had a smile! … I had brainwashed myself and repeated again and again that I am really a happy, happy, very happy person.

I became drunk with my happy, happy sayings. Feeling almost hypnotized with the words…"Happy, happy, happy me"… to be honest, God, it was more like a rainy, manic Monday. Whenever I didn't feel happy my "Happiness" Teacher scolded me and said, "You're thinking wrong! That it's all up to me to change my world and create my own happiness…that I was the center of my own universe. That I am a little God growing up to be a big God." But, I was taught as a kid that you were God, God.

So much guilt came upon me that I couldn't get into that happy, happy state of mind. I actually thought my head would explode from all the pressure to be happy. But, I kept paying my Happiness Teacher to be happy. I kept smiling and lying to myself that I was a happy, happy person. My teacher would not hear of negative talk…even if someone died…I was not allowed to mention it…it was too negative.

She would always say, "You're thinking wrong?" and made fun of me if I cried. She would say, "Boo, hoo"….as if I was back to being a baby trapped inside the house by another blizzard. More and more guilt developed inside of me. I felt like a tornado waiting to happen. There was so much stress in me to be an enormously happy person.

Things in my life were going so bad for me. I really felt guilty when my dentist told me that my teeth started falling out because of the stress. I started gaining weight, too. The pressure was too much for me…after all, Happiness Teacher told me I was the creator of my own universe…a little God…growing up to be a big God. It was a lot of pressure!

Thanks to You… I found a twelve-step program for the weather!

Well, I left this "Happy, happy course" and was completely depressed. I was more miserable than when I started. So, I surrendered my happiness, trying to give everything over to a Higher Power. I lost my self-control in The "Happy course"… it was all about me, me, me, and I, I, I can make it happen. They made me feel like a magician. After all, thoughts are things…so thinking it will be making it happen. Well, it may work for someone else…but not for me. I left "Happy Land" and my Happy Teacher.

Now, I know that God. I am not the Creator of my universe…You are. You and only You created me for a higher purpose. Sometimes, it's clear…sometimes it's cloudy.

Like the weather...somedays are all sunshine and other days it's raining cats and dogs. I feel deeply without forcing myself to feel it... like the tears from my eyes that flow on my pillow when someone I love, dies. The pressure I gave myself to be "Happy" all the time almost led me to a nervous breakdown. You and only You have a Divine plan for my specific life. Your love is like an umbrella from the rain.

Please God, help me to survive the storm of life. Teach me to trust You and live in the moment...and see You through the clouds in every moment of my life.

Thank you for releasing me from the crazy human course of "Happy, happy thinking." Let my life flow naturally. It's still hard for me to live in the moment...but all I can do is try and do the best I can and feel the calm of a gentle breeze.

Whether the weather is simple sunshine or another dreary day, please take my hand and help me to surrender to Your will.

Love, Beating the Blizzard in Bayonne, NJ

Letter **14**

A cheap friend

A cheap friend

> "YOU SHALL LOVE YOUR NEIGHBOR AS YOURSELF."
> – Galatians 5:14b

It's easy to make friends, but hard to get rid of them.

— <u>Mark Twain</u>

Dear God,

You say, "Love thy neighbor as thyself"...I'm not having a problem with my neighbor... I'm having a problem with a friend. I need patience to have this guilt removed. You created this friend...I'm not one to talk...but she believes the earth revolves around her. I need Your patience to have this guilt removed from how I feel about her.

Twice a year, my friends and I get together with her. We call her "Miss Me, Myself and I" or "El Cheapo" for short. In fact, El Cheapo actually has money, but she won't spend it— she owns apartment buildings, buys fancy cars, buys fancy jewelry, plays the stock market, but she can't buy lunch!

One year, we decided not to include her and she found out anyways and felt betrayed by us. Well...because of this guilt we ended up including her in our next get together. No matter how hard we try, she ruins it all the time. When we go to lunch, she never orders because she claims she's not hungry. Well, before we can get a slice of bread and butter...it's all gone because El Cheapo consumed all

82

of it. Then she takes food from our plates nibbling here and there. She gains at least twenty pounds every time we get together. If there are any leftovers it's gone immediately, eaten by El Cheapo.

Another thing…We have to pick her up because she doesn't like to drive. She said she felt guilty and she gave me a dollar once for all the years I've been driving her…she said it's for gas. I told her it wouldn't buy a candy bar.

If there's a parking meter …she's the first to run out of the car so she doesn't have to pay. She doesn't have a quarter for the meter, either?! She says she has to get to a bathroom real quick. We decided to go to a Museum…all of us wanted to take a tour. Not her…Me, myself and I refused. Instead of hearing her complaints…we gave in and let her run the show. One of the girls decided to buy a hot dog. El Cheapo asked if she could just have a small bite before she bought her own to see how it tasted. She doesn't know what small is…her second bite was an even bigger bite than her first.

El Cheapo decided she wouldn't smoke anymore because of some health reasons. Well, one of the girls in our group smokes…she grubbed cigarettes from her until the pack of cigarettes was almost gone. We have all this guilt and she has none. She thinks and believes the Earth, Sun, Moon, Stars and every planet revolves around her. Could you please remove this guilt? I really can't take her anymore. I know you created her and love her…but it doesn't look like she's ever gonna change. Even her husband lets her boss him around. Even her family can't take her, but they invite her for the holidays and dread every second of it. I know because all her relatives do nothing but call and complain to me about how she has to have everything her way.

You know what? I decided I'm changing my telephone number and give the guilt to You, God. You're much stronger than I am. My patience is gone with Your creation of El Cheapo. When the group of us have our get togethers next time, I'll just say… "I can't make it"… and leave the suffering to my friends. Life is too short for this kind of aggravation.

Forgive me. Please send help to my friends and remove this guilt from me.

Love, A Frustrated Friend from Philly

84

Letter 15

Italian Mothers

Italian Mothers

ITALIAN MOMS
are better than the CSI
They know you did it,
how you did it,
whom you did it with,
and they can hear you
trying to hide the
EVIDENCE.

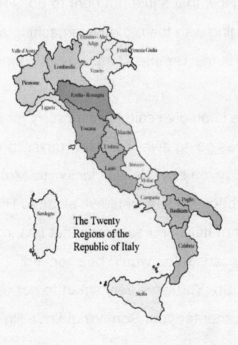

The Twenty
Regions of the
Republic of Italy

Dear God,

I was reading your book the other day... You know, the Bible... My Mother says it's a book of instructions of how to live a life of respect for your elders.

I know You and Your Son know everything ...at least that's what I've been told since I was a kid.

Your Son really frightened his mother, Mary, when he was away for those two days or so — she didn't know where He was so she must have been scared. Now that's just not right to do! I realize He was hanging with the old guys preaching and teaching in the Temple to the elderly... I mean "the Elders" —

He should've said He was sorry for not telling her He was going away for a few days...but He didn't. Boy, oh boy, He was lucky His Mother wasn't Italian ...because she would've slapped Him ...and said a lot of Italian curse words that I cannot repeat to You because You would be shocked!

So, You were very smart to not choose an Italian Mother for your Son. What I'm tellin' You is the truth. I'm Italian and if I ever spoke to <u>my</u> Mother like that, she would've killed me.

Love, Harry from Hoboken

Letter 16

Cracks in the sidewalk

Cracks in the sidewalk

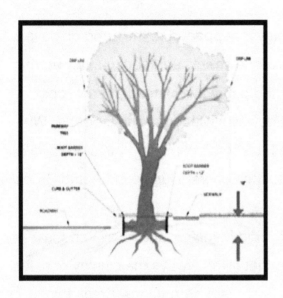

Dear God,

Whatever happened to the good ol' days with the cobble stone streets and soft, warm, weather with tree-lined parkways instead of hard, cold, concrete sidewalks with cracks in them...? Why does there have to be cement in the sidewalks? Welcome to the concrete jungle of LA and Brooklyn, too!

Well, I did it again... the ol' slip and fall. My Father said that I was always the clumsy one. It's also all his fault that I drop things, break things, and lose things almost everyday.

I don't look where I'm going and walk into walls. I trip when I walk. Why don't they just create padded sidewalks? At least when I fall at home, I have padded rugs...so if I fall, I bounce right back up.

I'm not the only one who trips on cracks in the sidewalks. Almost all my friends trip on the cracks in the sidewalks. You can ask them and they'll tell you their problems and how they all got hurt from cracks in the sidewalks.

There should be signs warning people about the cracks in the sidewalks. Maybe there should be a protest about sidewalks altogether. "WE want padded sidewalks! no more hard, cold, cracked, cement…!!!"

I realize now my earthly Father was wrong. What he forgot to tell me was after falling, comes the gorgeous greeters of this damsel in distress … who knew "perfect pecs" came with every paramedic who comes to your rescue! Their bulging biceps and tight uniforms made them even cuter! I'm literally bleeding out through my nose and they're seeing me at my absolute worst, but I didn't care… I wanted to take them out to dinner anyways. "It's not my fault…it's the sidewalk's fault," I told them.

Sidewalks are still dangerous, but the thought of a perfect paramedic rescuing you almost makes it worth it!

Love, Concrete Connie from Coney Island.

Letter 17

Super Religious person

Super Religious person

I'm not lucky... You have no idea how much I've prayed.

Dear God,

There's lots of movies out now breaking box office records with comic book super heroes and even some movies about super hero animals, too, but what about real-life super religious persons... what about them?

Now, most people have seen "All Dogs Go To Heaven," and some people have even met the Dali Lama, but let me tell you ...I met a Super Duper religious woman at church and she thinks she's starring in her own movie... if You know what I mean...!!! She's more like a figment of her own imagination...!!!

She considers me like a daughter... Mom #2 is what I call her. Well ...that was my first mistake. I got way too close to her, but what can you do? She said, "the waiting for God is over and that God is coming back soon." I hope not too soon, I'd still like to finish my bucket list, God.

Anyway, as I said before, Mom #2 is super religious. She doesn't really know the Bible (as good as she think she does), but she follows all the people who see visions and think they are hearing these messages from, You, God.

95

Now, this woman claims she got a revelation from God and that God told her: He'll be coming back soon. She told me, the woman gave her specific instructions on what we "must do" to be saved. So, my Mom #2 told me that we need to drive to San Francisco and buy a row boat. A row boat... I haven't thought about a row boat since that summer camp song... you know, "row" it gently down the stream...!

Well, are you ready for the next part... then, wait til you hear this— she said we have to tie the row boat to a tree and we have to get in it ...because it'll be the end of the world and being in the row boat, we'll be saved.

Mom #2 means a lot to me. I respect her. I'm a responsible person. I cannot leave (this earth) without paying my bills, leaving everyone and just hanging out in a row boat doesn't make sense to me. We've all been waiting for You to return so we can go to heaven and stop paying taxes, too! What do you think?

Love, One Oar Out of the Water in Oyster Bay, NY

Letter **18**

Problems with teenage sons

Problems with teenage sons

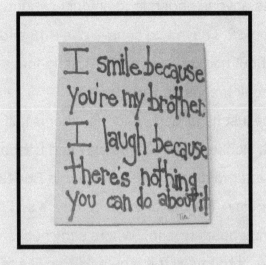

I smile because you're my brother. I laugh because there's nothing you can do about it
Tia.

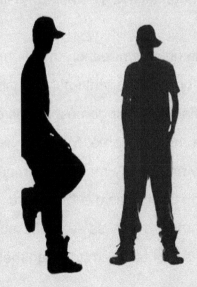

Dear God,

Does anyone understand anything about teenage boys? I have two sons— one's 13 and worries about hair gel the other is 15 and focuses on his Facebook friends and Twitter.

One just hit puberty and the other is half way through it. Hockey game is Tuesday and Baseball is Friday. Band practice is Wednesday and Boy Scouts is on Thursday. Neither of them can drive so I'm mother and chauffeur, too. Where's my husband, their father, through all this You ask... I'd like to know that too, God!

For some unknown reason they fight about everything and I mean everything! My husband is a referee on the field for their games, but he can't get in the middle of them at home! We both have jobs with the County and barely make ends meet! When I get home, I can't be the maid— but, I am.

Their rooms are a mess as if a bomb hit them. How many times do I tell them to clean their rooms but they don't listen.
Their dad runs into his bathroom like a kid himself, every time they fight because he can't handle them.

99

I, on the other hand, appear to be able to handle it all — Not so much. I'm really really getting frustrated. When I was 19, I gave up singing and dancing with a thriving career in the arts to get married and start a family. Patience is a virtue, I know; but, how can I have patience when I'm screaming and yelling all the time at them? Can you give me some (more) patience... and I need it now!

One other thing while I'm at it. I am also a human Parrot. I have to repeat and repeat and repeat myself to my sons and my husband. None of them listen... check that, they only hear what they want to hear. Listening is not their strong point.

The only one that is good to me is my golden retriever, Ruby. My dog loves me and listens to me. Ruby is so patient and loves me, unconditionally. You're really good at that unconditional love thing, too, God.

How do I get my 3 boys to listen to me without screaming at them all the time... even some of the time? Can you hear me God over all this screaming and yelling...?! Where and how do I get the gift of

patience? Help me! Save me! I'm trying to be a good Mother, but I think I'm going insane.
 Love your child, Concetta from Chicago

Letter 19

People who lie

People who lie

> Never lie to someone
> who trusts you.
> Never trust someone
> who lies to you.

TELL A LIE
ONCE
AND ALL YOUR
TRUTHS
BECOME QUESTIONABLE

Dear God,

Why didn't I know now what I should've known then? I could've...should've...would've done everything different if I could've figured out people who lie. I was raised to trust people. Who knew that so many people lie and cheat. How can I tell when people lie to me?

Do I need patience to find out about liars? I can't believe I could be so naive and believe when someone is lying to me. They must have no conscience. Just because I meet people at church doesn't mean that they're not going to lie, too.

They look like Saints when they're praying and as soon as they're done they tell me their sad story. All of a sudden, they turn to me and say: "You look like a person I could trust." Then, I'm trapped. ...I mean really I'm trapped — trapped into believing this fairy tale horror story of their lunatic life...and then, they ask me to help them and give them, money... "just this one time...!"

They want me to just help them because by next week all will be different...the money will come in …or they will have the check in the mail…It's like they are wolves in sheep's clothing.

Why do they come to me… do I have some sort of a sign hanging on my back that reads: "GO TO HER…SHE'LL BELIEVE ANYTHING."

Could you change me…? Help me to be more discerning…and be sharper like some other people I know. Even my teenage nieces and nephews are not fooled like I am…!!!

How long does it take for me to have discernment? Is discernment like patience, God, because I need some now! I'm not that young anymore. I always think the person is telling me a true story! I am hurt because now, I'm the brunt of the joke… they got me to give them money and that's no joke!!!

Help me please to be able to see people more crystal clear…so I can one day say, "Ah ha… that person is lying and trying to get me to give him some money… do I look like a bank?!…"

Love, Penniless in Poughkeepsie

Letter 20

Seeking "Mr. Right" in Rome

Seeking "Mr. Right" in Rome

Dear God,

First, I want to thank You and Your Mother for helping me save enough money to get to Europe. My purpose was to meet "Mr. Right" and get married. The cruise as you know did not work for me. Hanging over the rail on a ship is not very romantic. With all the high waves, a rocky boat and a fishy smell ...well, you know the rest. It did not work out according to my plan.

So, off to Europe ...waiting patiently in the long line to catch the plane ...up in the air and here we go along with all the birds. Why is it so much work to travel? You gave me a stomach that can't drink alcohol or coffee when I'm flying. In the movies, they all look so great eating and drinking ...and in the old movies smoking, too. Why do I have to get sick on a plane? Is my life going to be lived in the world of cement?

Anyhow, It's "Romantic in Rome"... I met a friend at the Vatican who told me someone just stole his camera there so I better watch out. What I loved about Rome was that it reminded me of "New York Italian Style"... I loved all the people in Rome —

moving fast, flirting, eating with "Michelangelo and his Art" all around me. Finally, I didn't feel lonely. Who had time to think of my loneliness when I saw so many "magnificent men made of marble" and "real" people moving and talking not just with their mouth but with their hands waving as if everyone was conducting an orchestra.

"Mr. Right" did not appear in Rome. So, off to Venice I went… I was seeing so many romantic photos of Venice that I was sure I'd meet him there. "My one and only" that I've waited for my whole life. Who knew the boat ride to Venice would make me sick?! Besides, the water smelled so bad …and, then, I saw huge rats. I've never seen such big rats in my life. I thought I saw them waving to us and wearing scarfs and hats just like Italians…but that had to be my imagination!

Finally, we arrived in Venice. I saw two friends I kind of knew who I met at the Vatican and asked them to join me in the Gondola. My goal was to get a man — any man— between us two girls, so I could feel the male presence in between us. I placed everyone in the Gondola …our fellow male friend in the middle (and he wasn't made of marble) — he was the real deal and we gals were by his side so he could hug us the whole ride. I just let myself be in fantasy for a moment. My fanciful, glamorous gondola ride finally became reality.

After the romantic ride, they went off their merry way and "Mr. Right" was no where in sight. But, Venice was so beautiful. The food was fantastic and beauty was all around me, but I was so lonely. I kept thinking ... "why didn't I go with a group of people instead of going alone?" I thought, "If I went with a group, they would rush from place to place, packing and unpacking…rushing here and there to see everything… getting their money's worth."

Besides, my hair bothered me …I should've brought a wig. It takes forever with the washing, drying and hot rollers …sometimes, my life doesn't make sense.

Seeking "Mr. Right" in Rome and Venice has exhausted me. Now, I think the problem is me … me being with me all day long is driving me crazy.

No wonder people stay married to people they don't like — at least they can blame their problems on each other and escape from reality. Look at Mark Antony and Cleopatra… that was love, real love and she killed herself with a snake. I can't stand snakes — poor Cleo— that must've hurt her real bad. Women love too much!

Okay, God, please know I want to thank You and Your Mother for all the traveling I've been doing …it didn't bring about "Mr. Right"…but I have fond memories of my trips and I appreciate it.

I tried seeking "Mr. Right" in Rome and all I got were sexy statues. Couldn't You give me a clue where he is so I don't have to keep spending all this money on traveling?

Love, Anna Maria in Manhattan

Letter 21

Confessing my guilt

Confessing my guilt

Dear God,

How do you put up with human beings? Well, today I should've received 10 Gold Stars for patience. I was waiting in line at Chuck & Charlie's Jewish Deli for the deal of the day.

Well, You would've been really proud of me. There I was smiling and being very nice to everyone. Then it was my turn. I ordered pastrami on rye with a side of mustard, cheddar cheese, and a Buy One Get One Free coupon for a pound of cold cracked pepper turkey at $11.68 per pound. Well, the deli counter clerk who waited on me made a mistake on the cold cracked pepper turkey. He undercharged me. The total was supposed to be $11.68... but, he only charged me $1.68. My Catholic guilt kicked in immediately— I couldn't just take the free cold cracked pepper turkey from the nice deli counter clerk and leave the deli and live with a guilty conscience. My life would've been consumed with guilt over a "coupon" for cold cracked pepper turkey.

So, I called the deli counter clerk over and explained my situation. "Excuse me, you undercharged me by $10.00 and since I'm Catholic with a lot of Catholic guilt already, could you <u>please</u> correct the total amount because I don't want to have to go to Confession over a BOGO coupon," I said.

Well, the man behind me who was waiting on line started complaining about me (out loud) so everyone else in line could hear him huffing and puffing. He turned to everyone else standing and waiting in line and said, "She has to correct the price…I'm tired and she has to feel the need to correct the price so now all of us have to wait in line even longer! You're Unbelievable, Lady!"

So, out of courtesy, of course, I felt the need to further explain myself. I had to tell him that I'm innocent here and I'm Catholic and I don't want to have to go to "confession" because of the coupon for cold cracked pepper turkey. So, I said, "Sir, I'm not in a hurry you can go ahead of me. I'll wait." Then, the impatient man said, "No, I insist, lady, even though I'm very tired and exhausted and I just got off the airplane, I'll wait. Please, you go."

Here, on planet earth, no one has patience. Maybe on another planet but…not Earth. Earth = NO PATIENCE!

So, here is my confession to you, God. I really wanted to say to him: "Sir, today is only Monday. If you only knew the pain of guilt that I had to live with for the rest of my life or at least until Saturday at Six when Father Frank is hearing confession… then, you would really understand the extent of the guilt that I will have to bear."

Even my Jewish friends understand Catholic guilt. There is something good about going to confession AND having a coupon for cold cracked pepper turkey.

Love, Dolly from DeKalb Avenue in Brooklyn

Letter 22

Seeking the "real" me

Seeking the "real" me

Dear God,

When I was a child, I didn't have "Keeping Up with the Kardashians" to watch. I had to wait impatiently to grow up and become the "real" me. So, when I was 10, I decided to be like my big sister...after all, she was tall and beautiful.

Then, I became a teenager and I needed to find the "real" me somewhere else. I saw this real pretty popular girl in our neighborhood... she lived a block away from me and she raised her eyebrows a lot. So, when I was 13, everyone noticed that I was raising my eyebrows a lot, too, but that thrill lasted only 1 week.

My family had no clue that I was seeking the "real" me...and I thought I found it if I could just be like that pretty girl in the mirror...but I had to raise my eyebrows to be pretty. I did it so much even my eyebrows got tired. I tried to be like so many other people that I even started talking differently. One day, I came home with a British accent and then I decided to dance by making a clicking sound with my mouth because a real pretty girl did that and all the boys liked her. She was so pretty, she came from the Bronx.

Believe me, God, it was hard work searching for the "real" me. Then from there, I went to magazines and movies to find the "real" me. So, when I was 16, I styled my hair like Natalie Wood in "West Side Story" the movie. I really liked my new hair-do but that thrill lasted only 2 weeks.

Then, I thought if I had the right clothes or maybe the right shoes…especially hand made leather boots I would find the "real" me. Cowboy Boots had so much personality…especially when cowboys wore them. So, when I was 22, I bought myself a pair of (cow girl) boots and that thrill lasted only 3 weeks. I could find myself in boots…that's the key…I thought. I was getting older…how long does it take to get to the "real" me.

Then, a light bulb went on inside my head… that's when I thought I found the answer, yet, again. So, when I was 33, I bought a white Cadillac Eldorado. When I drove it, I felt great and the "real" me was coming out for sure this time, but that thrill lasted only 4 weeks.

Then, buying a Condo was what I needed to make me happy and find the "real" me...yes, that's it! A home to call my own...fix it up...invite my family and friends over for dinner. So, when I was 39 (My "Forever" Birthday), I decided to buy the Condo but that thrill lasted only 6 weeks...back to my search for the "real" me.

Then, I figured the "real" me would pop out (for sure) if I just got married... and I could look like Marilyn Monroe in the fancy white dress... well, maybe not quite that fancy!

Well, I knew some friends that were happily married. So, when I was 41-ish, I decided to get married — that way, I wouldn't have to work anymore. My husband must be wealthy, of course, so he can pay all my bills...so, I can just be with him and we will travel the world and have all sorts of fun together.

So, I did meet a wealthy man and decided that I would love him...because he would bring out the "real" me for ever and ever.

I lied to myself and to him that I was madly in love with him...and he was the only one for me. But, this time, the lie caught up with me but that thrill lasted only 8 weeks.

I couldn't stop crying...I just kept crying...so, our relationship fell apart faster than I had put it together.

I was so empty inside. It was my plan, my way, my pride, my yearning to make it all happen the way I wanted it to happen...well, it didn't.

Do you know how exhausting it can be to find the "real" me...?!!!?

Love, Susie and Still Searching in Staten Island

Letter 23

Solving problems thru 12 Step programs

Solving problems thru 12 Step programs

GOD GRANT ME THE
SERENITY
TO ACCEPT THE THINGS
I CANNOT CHANGE
COURAGE
TO CHANGE THE
THINGS I CAN AND
WISDOM
TO KNOW THE DIFFERENCE

Dear God,

Wine is supposed to be good in moderation. I'm Italian. My Grandpa made his own wine so, wine went with every Italian meal. "A glass of wine a day keeps the Doctor away" was our family motto. Even the rich, red color is exciting!

Even more exciting was when I married a fun loving man who loved his wine. In fact, his whole family enjoyed wine. We had wine parties with our friends all the time. Somehow, my stomach couldn't take drinking wine anymore. So, I had to stop drinking. It was hard watching everyone have so much fun at our wine parties, while I now had to drink only soda.

I missed acting crazy. I missed my "hip, hip hooray" fun and, most of all, having the guts to sing — even though I couldn't sing. With one glass of wine, I would begin to sing "Somewhere Over the Rainbow" and try to sound like Judy Garland.

Do you remember when my Aunt took me aside and said I was an "enabler" to my husband and his friends... right there... during his birthday party? She even kinda got mad at me and said, "Don't you see anything wrong with them drinking wine all night when you have to clean up the mess after everyone else passes out?" Wow... was I confused or what. I thought that was normal... didn't everyone pass out after a few glasses of wine (well, maybe more than a few drinks)."

Well, that strict Aunt of mine told me to go to a 12 Step program for my problem. I didn't even know I had a problem...but Auntie was always the Boss to everyone in our family. She was a little frightening because she towered over all of us— always judging all of us and cursed at us in Italian. She was the biggest gossiper that I have ever known and I definitely didn't want her to gossip about me to my family and friends. So, I promised her that I would seek out a 12 Step program.

I immediately went on my computer to search for a 12 Step program. There were so may programs to choose from. There was "Clutterers Anonymous" that sounded like something I could use. I always had to clean up our home after the wine parties. I mean there was a lot of clutter around — especially wine bottles.

Then, I saw "Kleptomaniacs Anonymous"...
well, I'm not a Kleptomaniac...but, it sounded so
interesting. I really wanted to go to Bloggers
Anonymous... but, I don't Blog... I do know a friend
who blogs... she might be interested. I showed the
list to my Aunt because there were so many
programs...and I wasn't sure what course to take.

My Aunt who is like a General in the Army
glared at me and told me that I wasn't going to night
school...that this was a 12 Step program for people
who really need help. I didn't know I needed
help...but Auntie General made a direct command
that I must go to Al-Anon. I said, "What's Al-Anon?"
"Don't ask so many questions," she said, "just go
and be healed." Now I was even more confused...be
healed? What did she think I had...?!

Like an obedient niece, I started a 12 Step
program in Al-Anon. It seemed like a good course.
When I got to my first meeting, some people were
crying and some were laughing. They suggested that
I get a sponsor. So, I asked this sweet gal to be my
sponsor. I told her my Aunt said I should take this
course because I was an enabler.

My sponsor said, "Your Aunt... does she have a drinking problem?" I said, "No, none that I know of, but she has other problems." My sponsor said, "Then, why are you here?" I told her that I was here to take the 12 Step course, I mean program.

"Well, does anyone in your life drink a lot," she asked. Then, I said, "Of course, my husband and all of his friends drink a lot of wine and pass out." She replied, "You need help!" I was so excited because that's what the General, I mean, my Aunt had said, too!

Al-Anon was quite a program and my sponsor was great. Other than that I enjoyed the stories and felt I had less problems because some of their problems were even bigger than mine. I reported back to Auntie General that I had done everything that she had told me to do and joined Al-Anon.

Then, she told me that I had to attend AA meetings. I told her that would be easy because I already belonged to AA — the American Airlines Frequent Flyer program and I only needed 10,000 more miles to get to Gold status... for life. She just looked at me and shook her head, "It's a different AA meeting — it's about drinking problems. Your husband has a disease."

My husband didn't have a disease. I mean, he's pretty healthy except when he passes out from drinking too much. After awhile, the AA meetings were so much fun. Everyone was so expressive. I had no idea so many people liked to drink. It was an education. I did learn one thing from both programs. The 12 Step program can help anyone. Next time, I think I'm gonna try the clutter course... I mean program.

Love, Always Anonymous in Albany

Letter 24

My secret addiction to chocolate

My secret addiction to chocolate

A
BALANCED
DIET IS
CHOCOLATE
IN BOTH
HANDS

Dear God,

I have a Secret...but, I think everyone is on to me. I have an addiction and it's getting worse. I don't smoke, drink or take drugs. Chocolate is my addiction!

I am a chocoholic and my life has become unmanageable. How long do I have to wait to out grow this chocolate addiction? I'm in my mid-30s, now. It all started in my early 20s. When I was a kid, I liked chocolate, but as I grew up, I loved chocolate.

Does chocolate addiction run in families? Maybe there should be a new 12 Step program called "Adult Children of Chocoholics." I heard that alcohol addiction runs in the family. They say it's in the genes. I don't remember anyone with an addiction to chocolate in my family, but me. Being Italian, I could see sauce and cheese addictions, maybe even salami addictions...but (not) chocolate!

Do you know that I was hiding a box of chocolates in the freezer? While watching TV, all I could think about was the hidden box of chocolate in the freezer. I sat there thinking to myself, "Did I put the chocolate between the broccoli and peas or was it the squash and the zucchini?"

When I had joined Weight Watchers, they said I could have a piece of chocolate per day...that only weighed one ounce.

So, I took out my Weight Watchers scale and weighed the piece of chocolate and ate it. Well, I thought I was cured for sure of my addiction because I put the rest of the box of chocolate back in the freezer and started watching television, again.

Well, the TV show was so boring and the chocolate was still in the freezer. So, I went back to the refrigerator and I opened the freezer just to look and see the chocolate for a moment. Then, I opened the freezer again and decided to weigh another piece of chocolate.

Bravely, I thought another piece of chocolate couldn't hurt me. So, with courage of a soldier, I placed the box of chocolate back inside the freezer— making sure I would get a final whiff and sniff of the great smell of chocolate.

Then, I slowly closed the freezer door. It was back to the boring TV show...trying to watch something interesting to stop me from inhaling the rest of the box of chocolate. Well, I went remote control clicker crazy…changing and changing channels and becoming a fanatic, continually changing channels with my clicker. Then, I swung my chair around and started watching the refrigerator…focusing on the freezer. It was as if I had X-Ray vision and could see the box of chocolate and even smell it.

By the time the TV show was over, I had been opening and closing the freezer door so much that the hinges were getting loose from continually checking the chocolate. I couldn't contain myself anymore. Then, I almost ripped the freezer door off by grabbing the entire box of chocolate while weighing and eating each piece and ate all of them.

How do people eat just one piece and not hear chocolate talking to them in their head…?! Chocolate has a very distinct voice. I know that voice. First, it tells me to smell the chocolate. Then, take a small bite. Now, the chocolate and I have become one!

Whenever I buy chocolate, I try to convince the salesperson that I'm buying it for other people. Not me. I lie to the person behind the counter and try to look innocent because I'm guilty. That way, they won't know the truth.

My heart is always pounding when I finally give my order, making sure they don't suspect it's (all) for me. So, I then try on my innocent face with a sincere smile. I hear "Next"…and it's my turn.

I tell the salesperson, "Oh, I'll have that piece…make it four of them for my mother and then, I think, my cousin would like eight pieces of that dark chocolate with the marshmallow inside…maybe they'll try this kind, too. So, please put 9 pieces of chocolate covered pistachios in there for my uncle and my aunt Connie would love a dozen of caramel clusters."

After all this, the salesperson asked me if I would like a free sample of chocolate. So, I took a deep breath and lied to the salesperson and made an announcement loud enough so everyone in the candy store could hear me say in my martyr like tone of voice…"Oh, no thank you. I don't eat chocolate. I'm visiting my family and I'm buying chocolate for them...and not for me... because as I said, I don't...in fact...I never touch the stuff."

Because of my guilt, I made sure I put all the blame on everyone else but me. It's very important to me that when I leave the store I can feel them saying, "Wow, how does she do it? Now, that's a brave woman who can buy all that chocolate for others and not one piece for herself. What strength...what courage...what a gal. I wish I could be just like her."

I imagined myself as Joan of Arc — leaving the candy store with a box of chocolates on my white horse.

Well, my chocolate addiction got worse...so I had to go for help...I went to "The Center for Chocoholics" and it cost me $500.00 to be released from my chocolate addiction. There, I joined their Chocolate Therapy group. It was a waste of money. I still craved chocolate.

So, I prayed and promised myself that for my New Year's resolution, I wouldn't smell or even take a bite of chocolate for one whole year!

I really did it. I finally gave up chocolate for an entire year! Feeling I was cured and freed of any more chocolate addiction, I decided to celebrate, making sure I would only weigh one ounce of chocolate and have just that one piece per day.

Then, I took one bite of chocolate— the music was back, the birds started singing, and romance was in the air. I started dancing and life was beautiful for a moment.

However, I couldn't take it anymore. It was just a matter of time before I went back to the binging, the hiding and the lying.

That one bite of that one piece of that one ounce of chocolate changed my life!

Love, Still Hiding Chocolate in Chelsea

Acknowledgements

Anne Bancroft

Dianne Crittenden

Bob Hope

William Liebling

Marty Litke

Walter Matthau

William S. Paley

Audrey Wood

Howard Zieff

Ron Scott

Jonni Hartman

W. Bruce Cameron

Rev. Robert T. Walsh, S. J.

SPECIAL THANKS

Paul Scott Adamo

Candice Azzara Family — and all my nieces, nephews, and godchildren

Justine Bateman and Jason Bateman

Meredith Baxter

Gary Busey

Sharon and Ron Carey

Mindy Cohn

Luis Cruz

Michael Damian

Djinna Gochis

Rev. John Hampsch

Kim Fields

Michael J. Fox

Gary David Goldberg

Mimi Gramatky

Michael Gross (and the Chicago nuns)

John Hamilton and Joe Hamilton Productions (JHP)

Sharon Lally

Loyola High School Class of 1978

Phil McKeon and Nancy McKeon

Aaron Mendelsohn and WGAW Publicity & Marketing Committee

Rob Newhart and Bob Newhart

Nichelle Nichols

Carroll O'Connor

Rosemary Oh

Rev. Tony Scannell

Rev. Daniel Ryan, S.J.

Patt Shea and Jack Shea

John Stamos

Irwin J. Tenenbaum, Esq.

Dick Van Patten

Lisa Whelchel

Tina Yothers

CPSIA information can be obtained
at www.ICGtesting.com
Printed in the USA
FSHW021622311018
53433FS